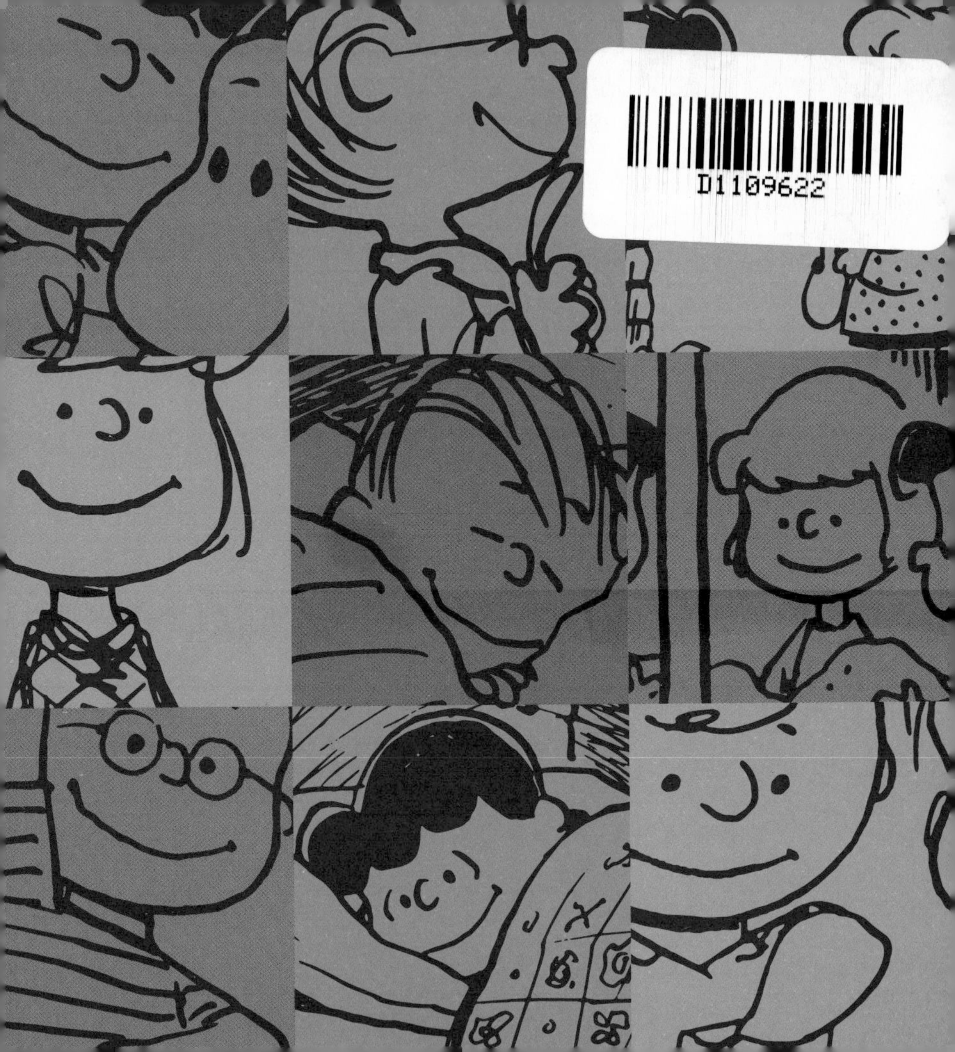

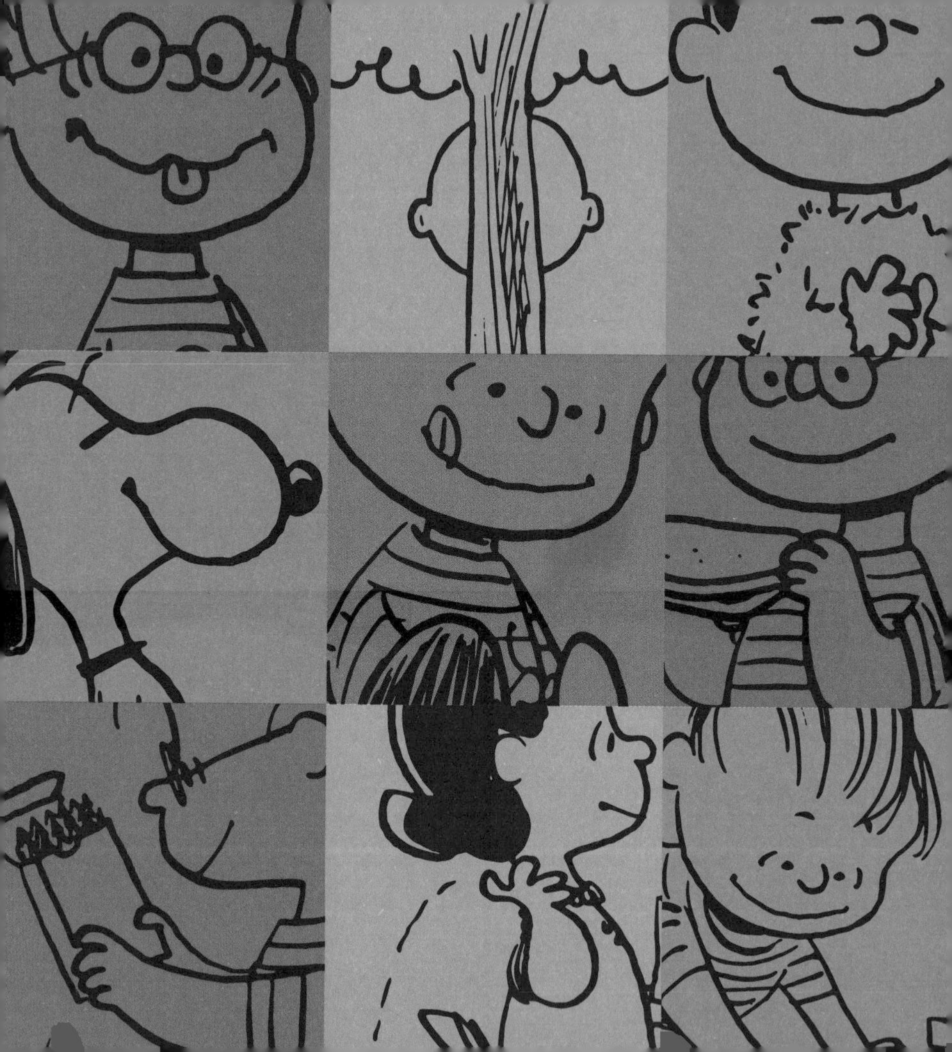

Happiness is
a Warm Puppy

ISBN-13: 9781604335767
ISBN-10: 1604335769
This book may be ordered by mail from the publisher.
Please include $4.50 for postage and handling.
But please support your local bookseller first!
Books published by Cider mill Press Book Publishers are available at special
discounts for bulk purchases in the United States by corporations, institutions, and
other organizations. For more information, please contact the publisher.
Cider Mill Press Book Publishers
"Where good books are ready for press"
12 Spring St.
PO Box 454
Kennebunkport, Maine 04046
Visit us on the web!
www.cidermillpress.com
Design by Jon Chaiet
Printed in China
1 2 3 4 5 6 7 8 9 0
First Edition

Happiness is a Warm Puppy

BY CHARLES M. SCHULZ

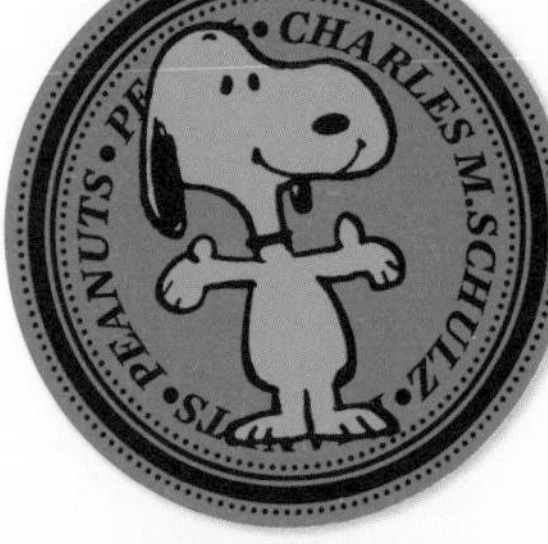
CHARLES M.SCHULZ
PEANUTS

**Happiness is
a thumb and a blanket.**

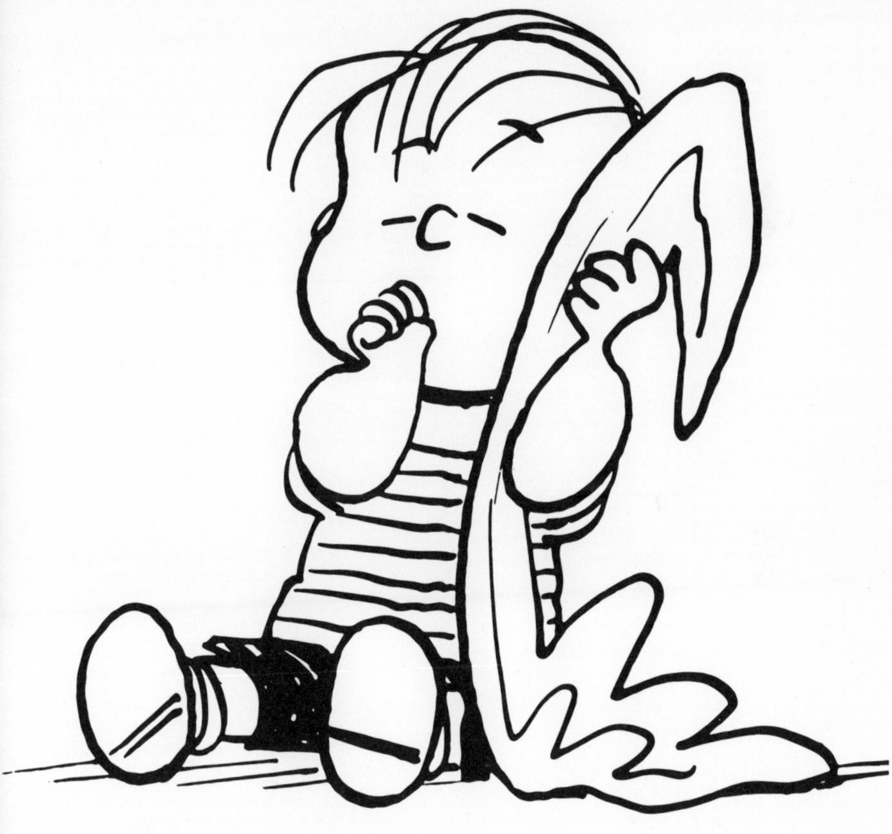

**Happiness is
an umbrella and
a new raincoat.**

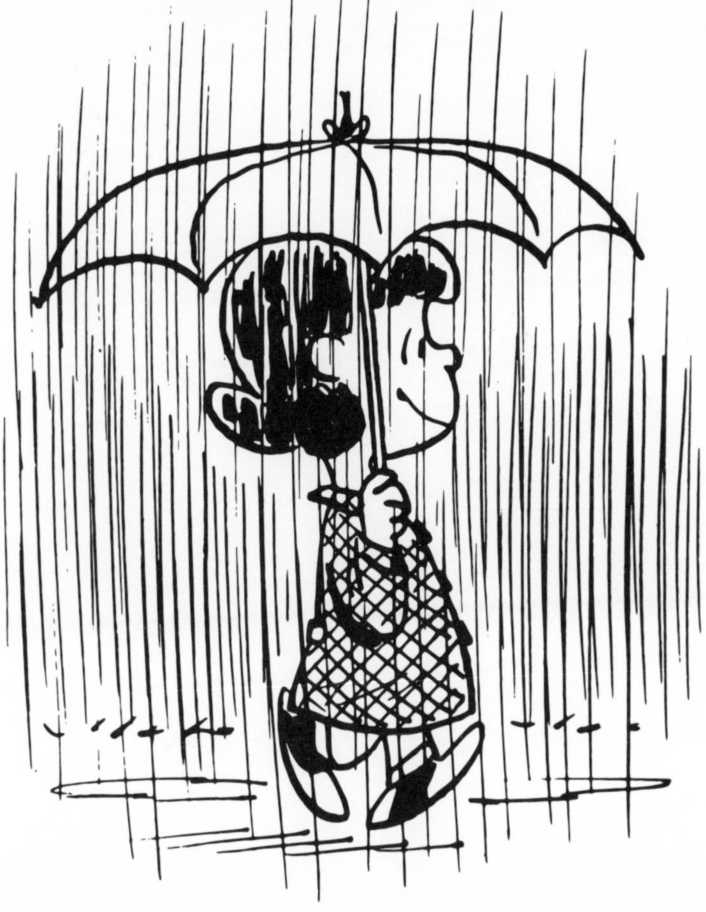

Happiness is a pile of leaves.

Happiness is a warm puppy.

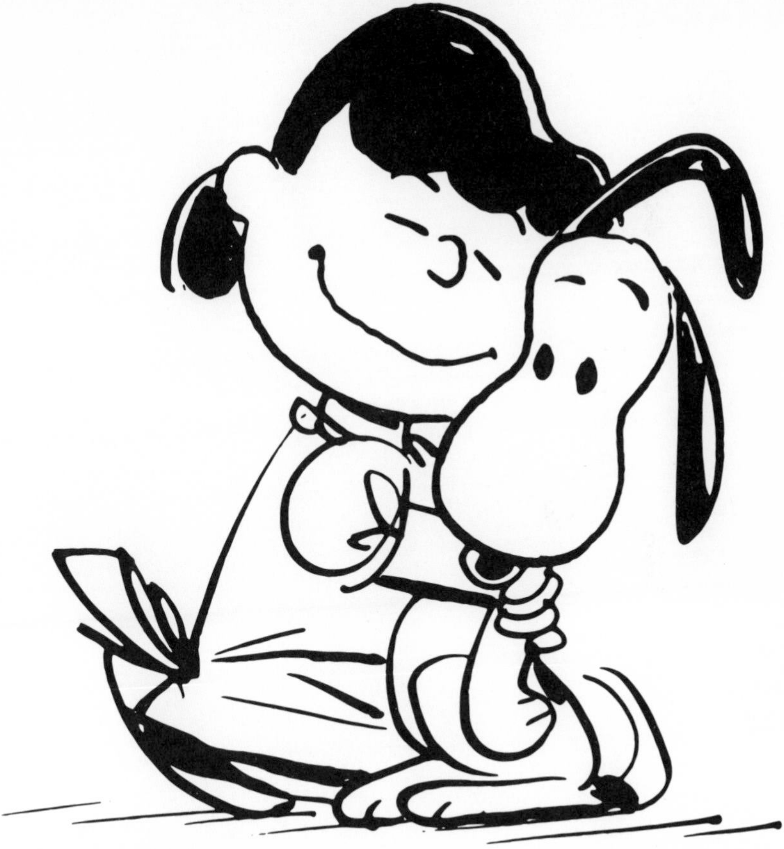

Happiness is
an "A" on your spelling test.

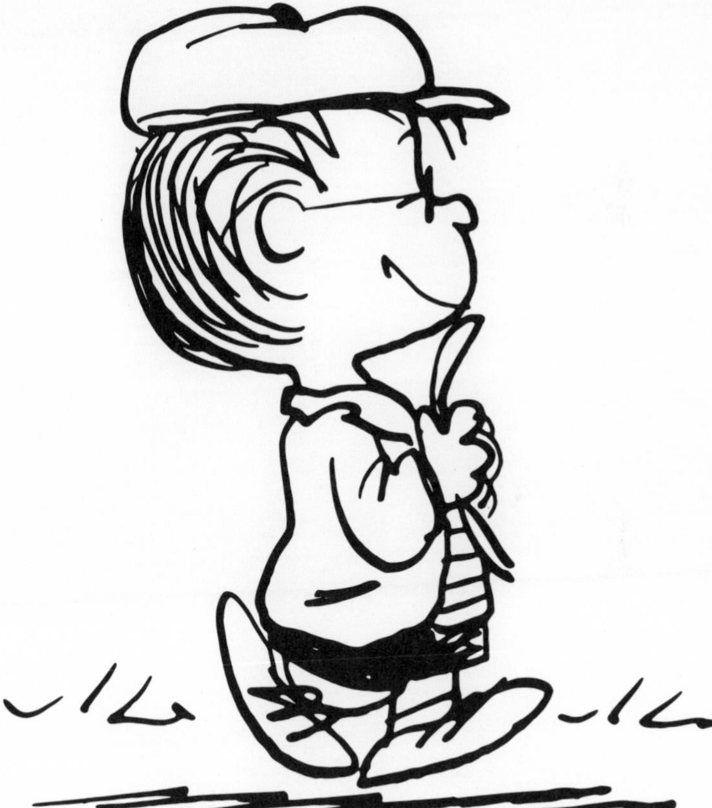

Happiness is finding someone you like at the front door.

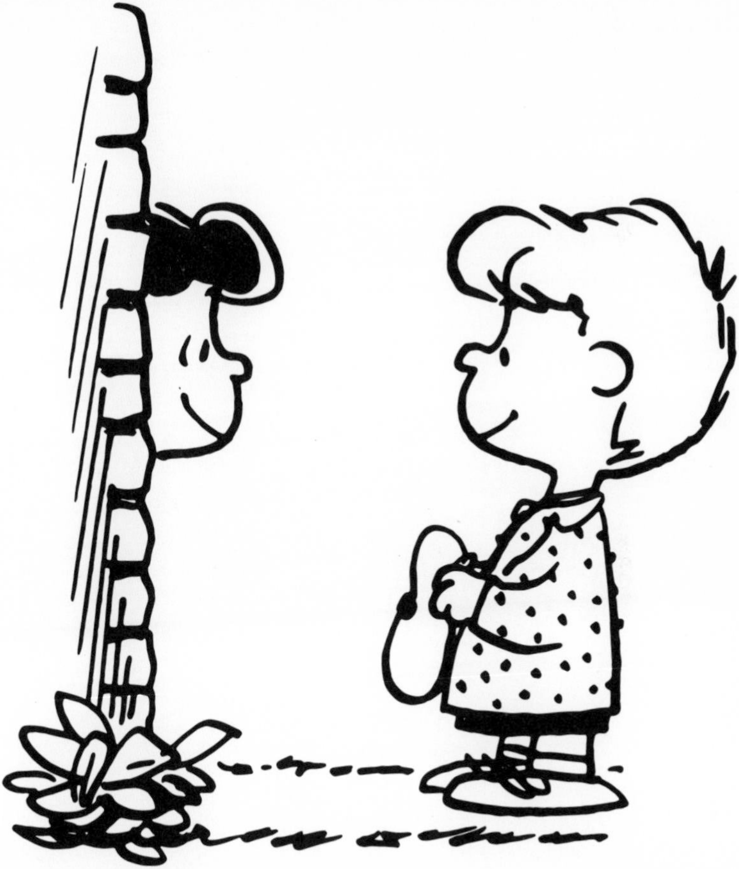

Happiness is
three friends in a sandbox...
with no fighting.

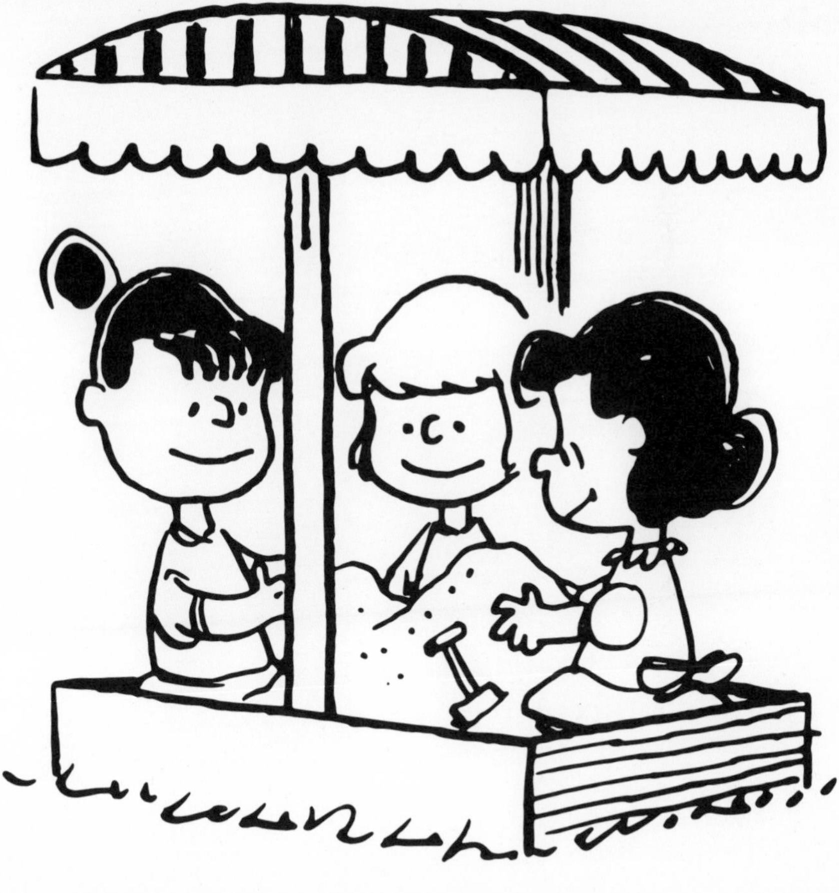

Happiness is
sleeping in your own bed.

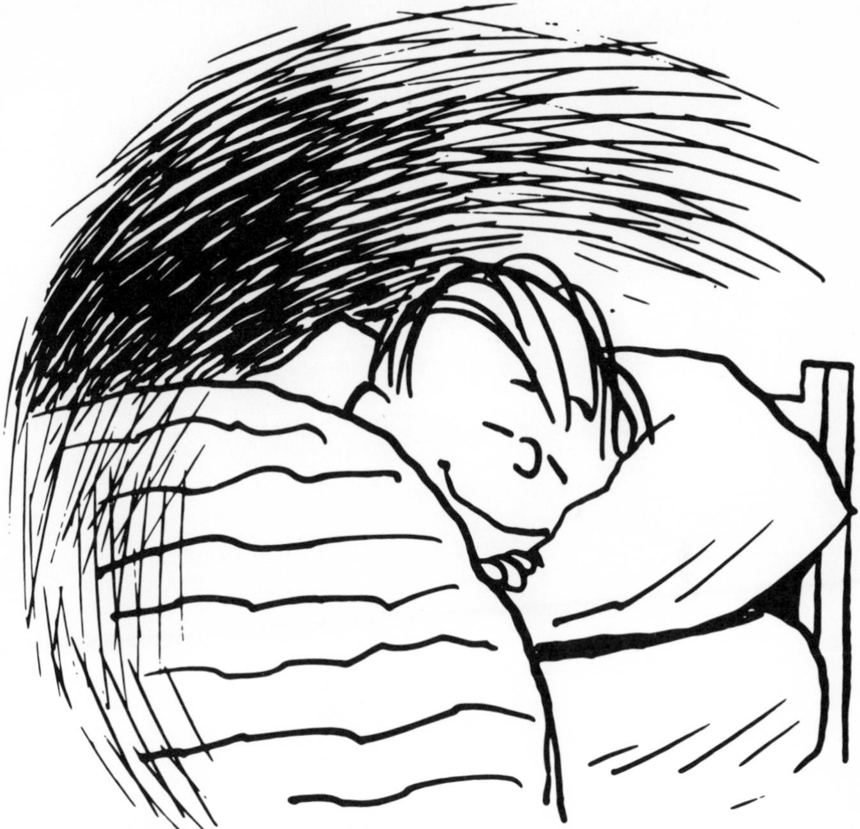

**Happiness is
a chain of paper clips.**

Happiness is getting together with your friends.

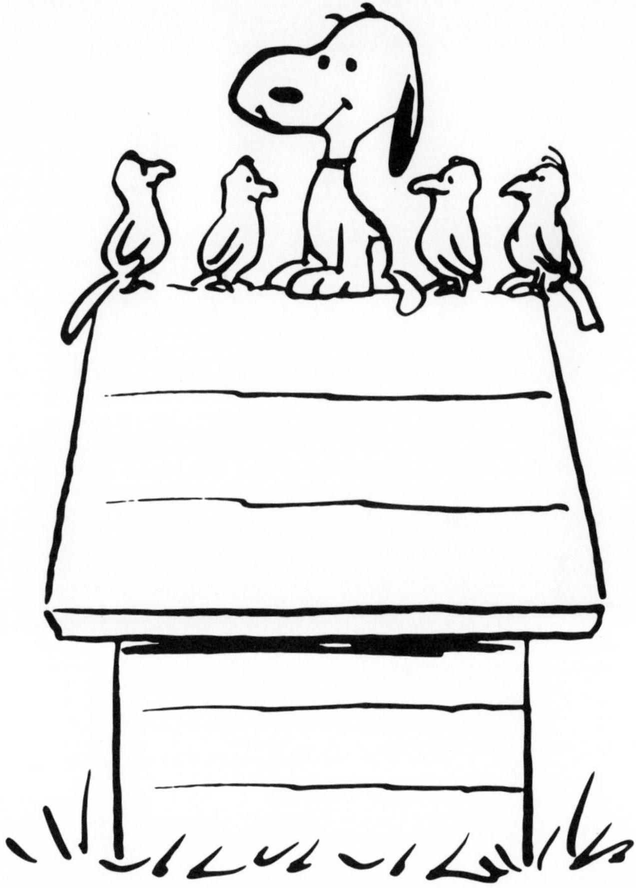

**Happiness is
a smooth sidewalk.**

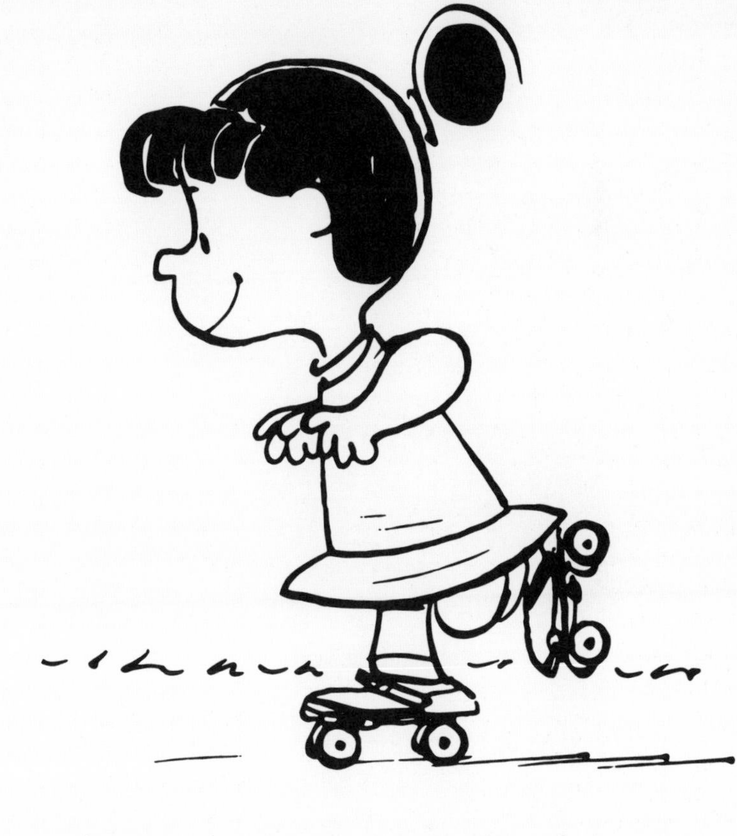

Happiness is finally getting the sliver out.

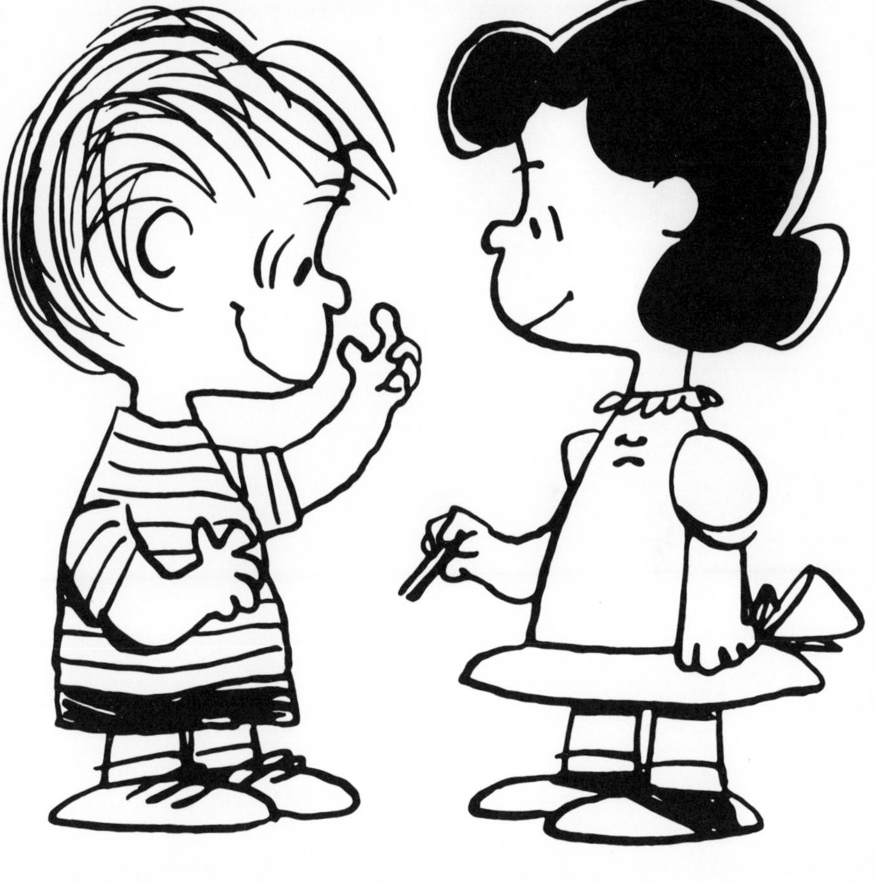

Happiness is a climbing tree.

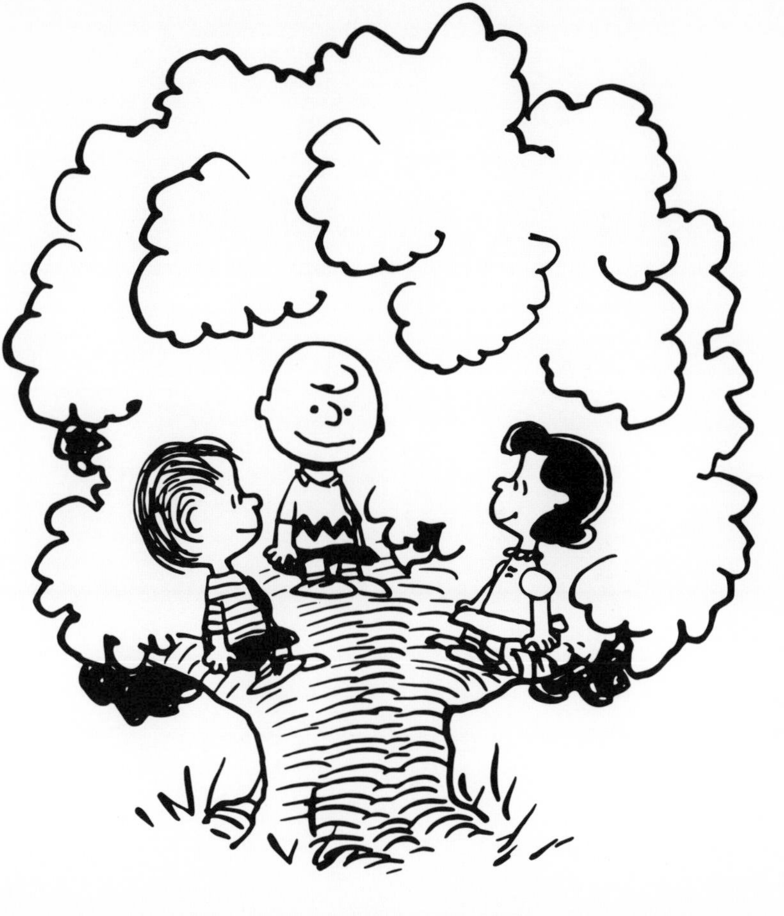

Happiness is lots of candles.

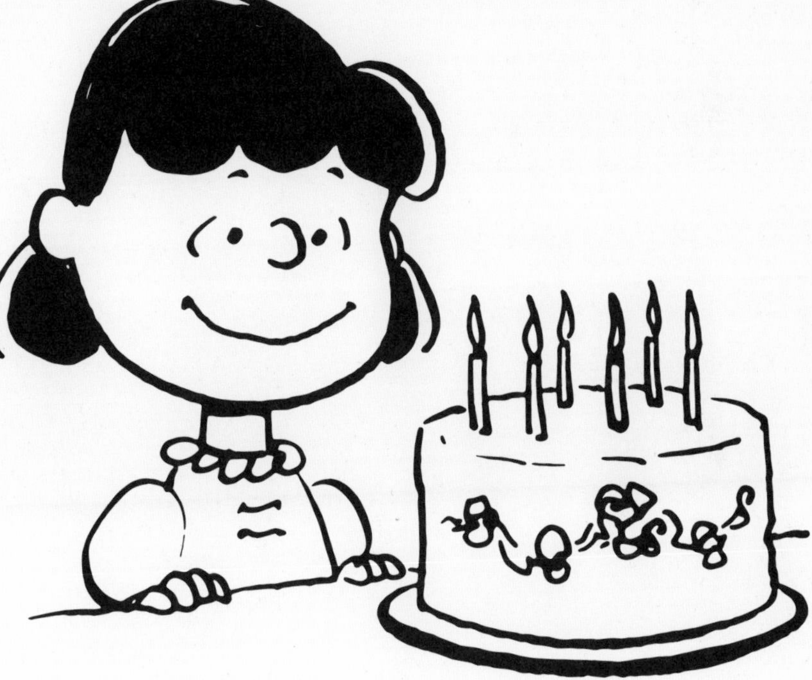

Happiness is being able to reach the doorknob.

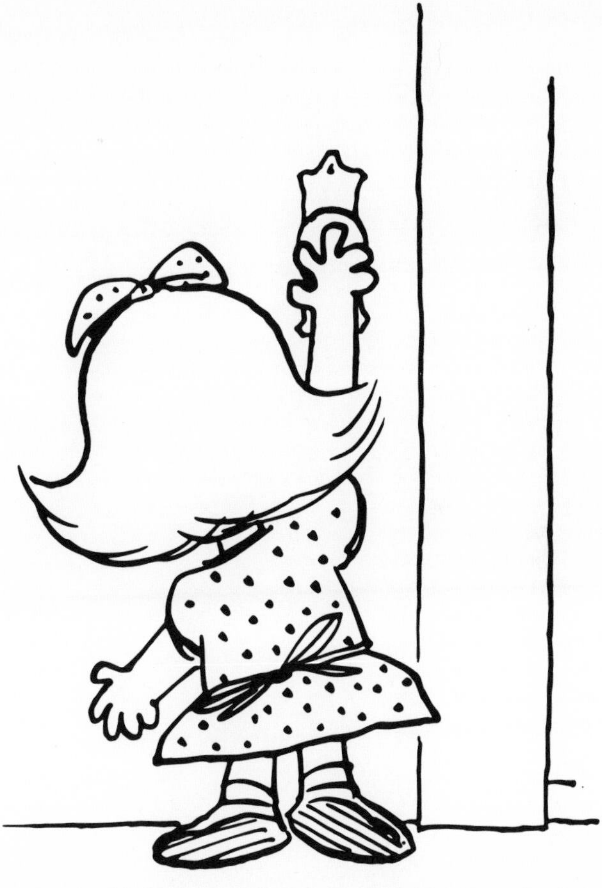

**Happiness is
knowing all the answers.**

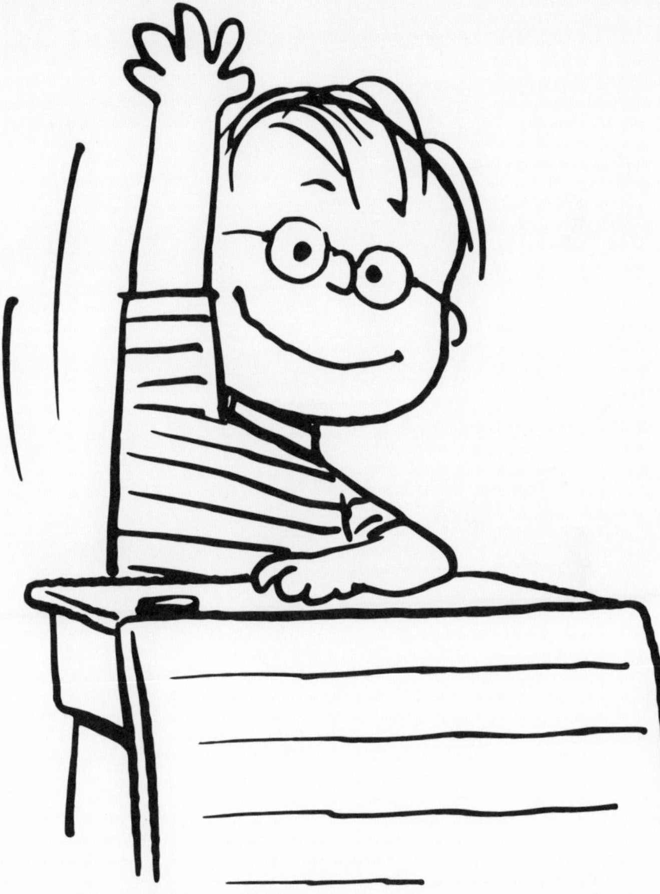

Happiness is a night light.

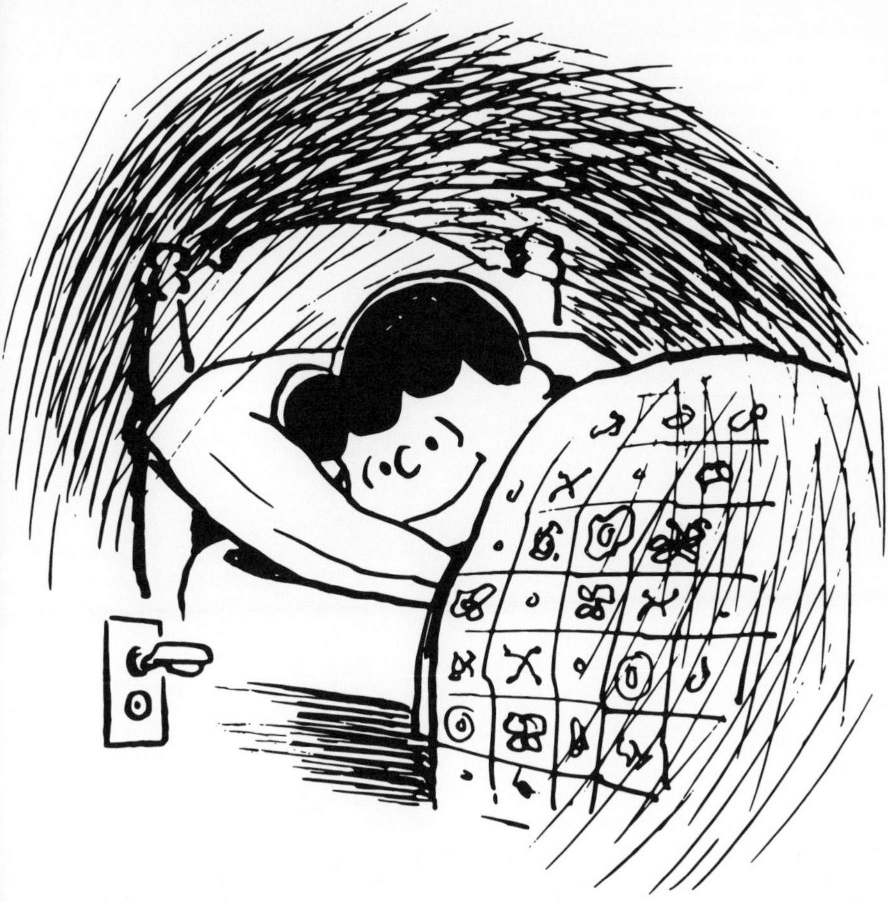

Happiness is
some black, orange, yellow,
white and pink jelly beans,
but no green ones.

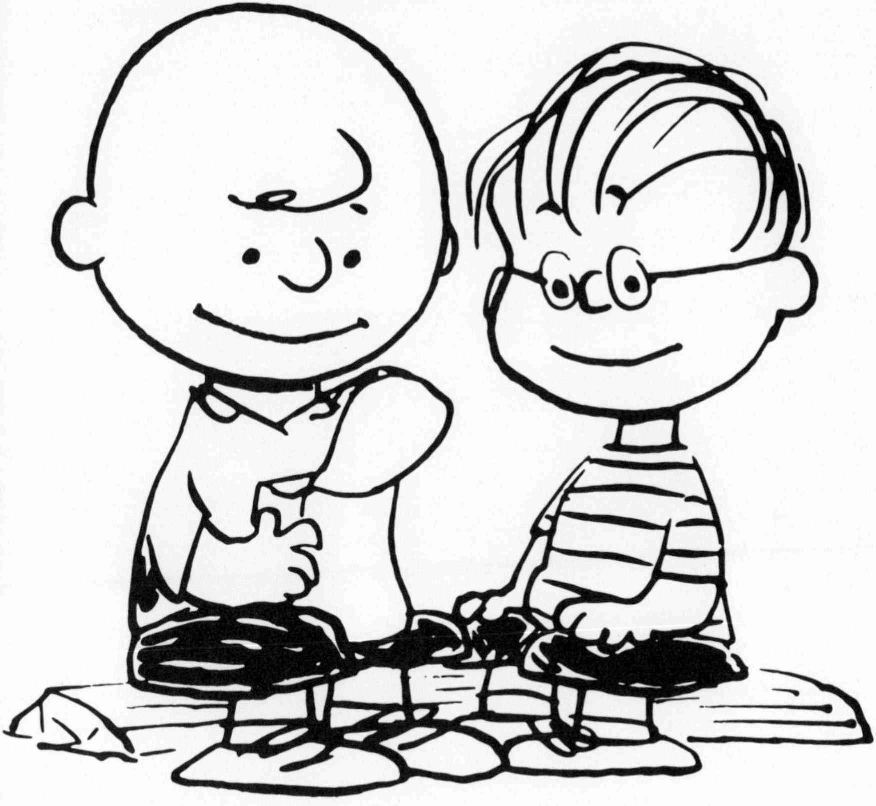

**Happiness is
the hiccups... after
they've gone away.**

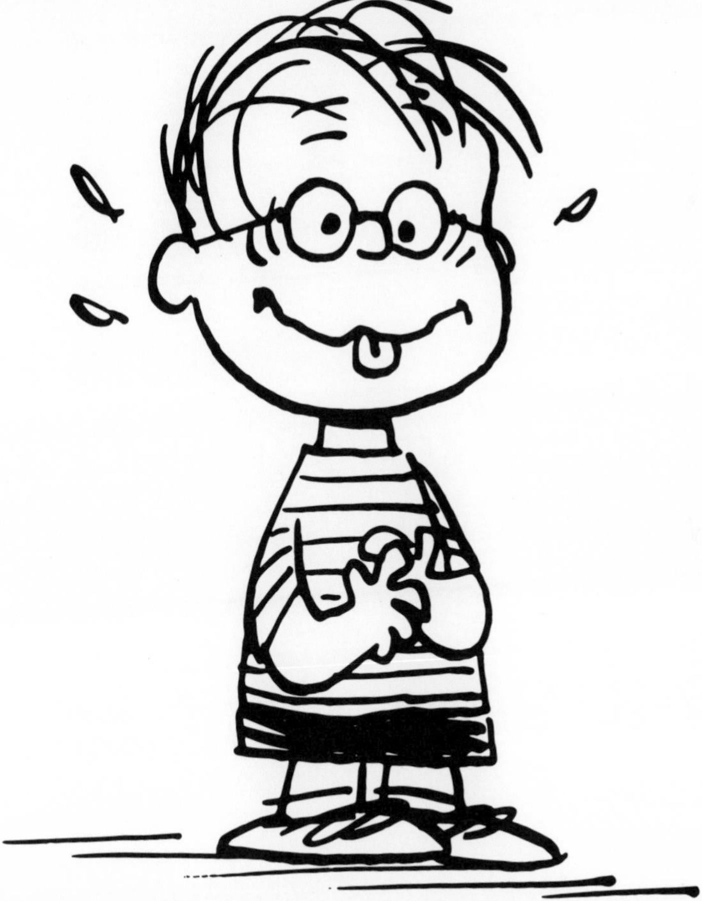

**Happiness is
a good old-fashioned
game of hide and seek.**

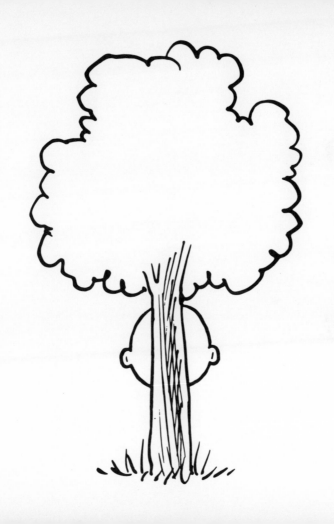

Happiness is a fuzzy sweater.

**Happiness is
a bread and butter
sandwich folded over.**

Happiness is knowing how to tie your own shoes.

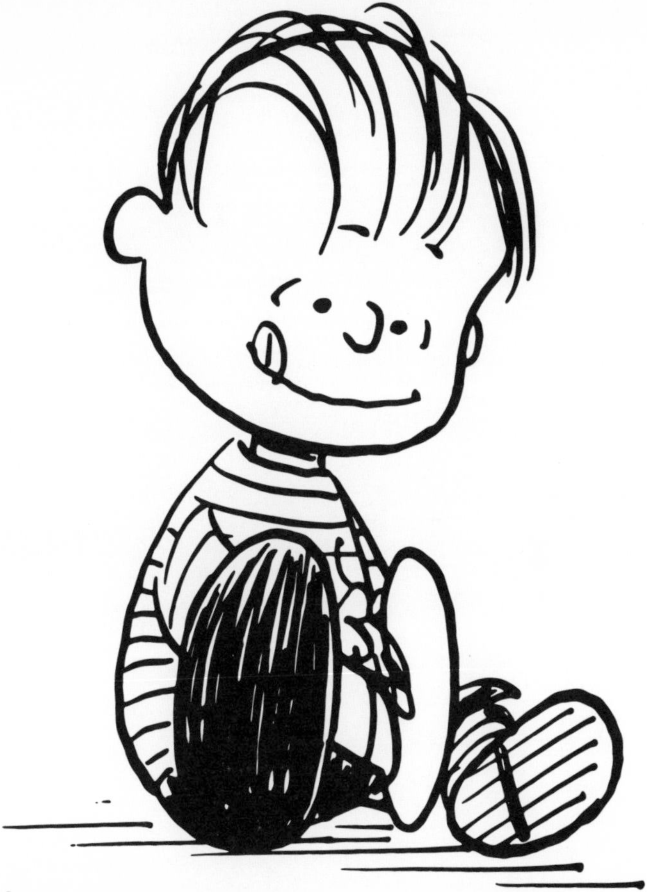

Happiness is
walking in the grass
in your bare feet.

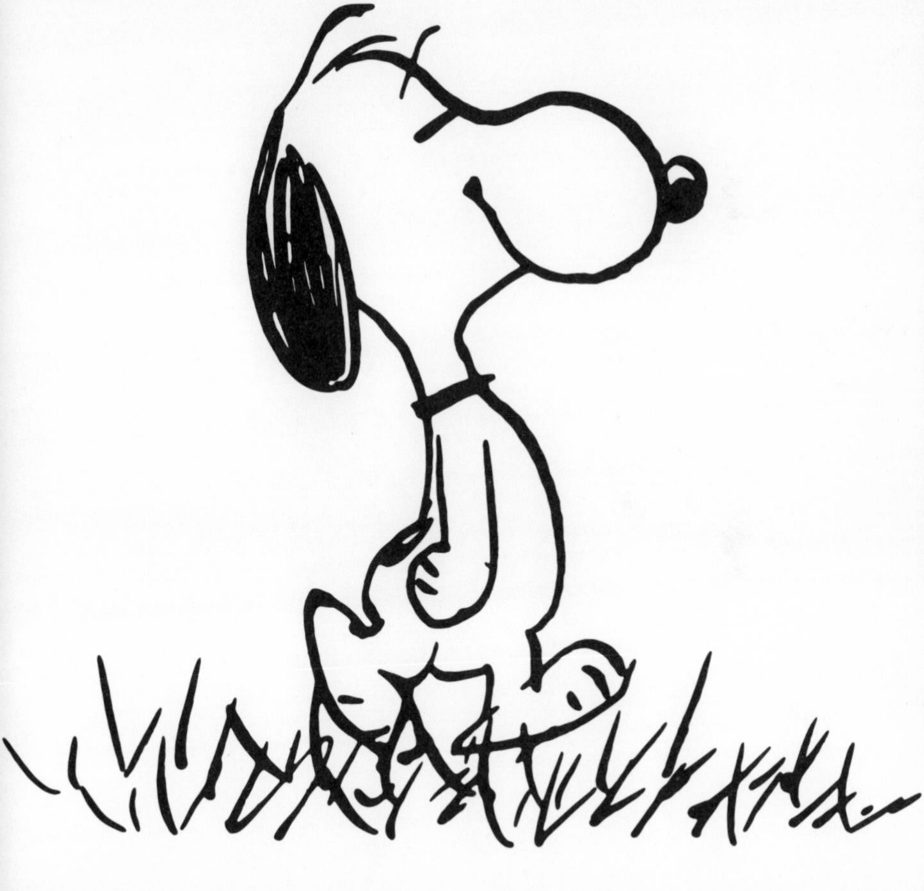

**Happiness is
eighteen different colors.**

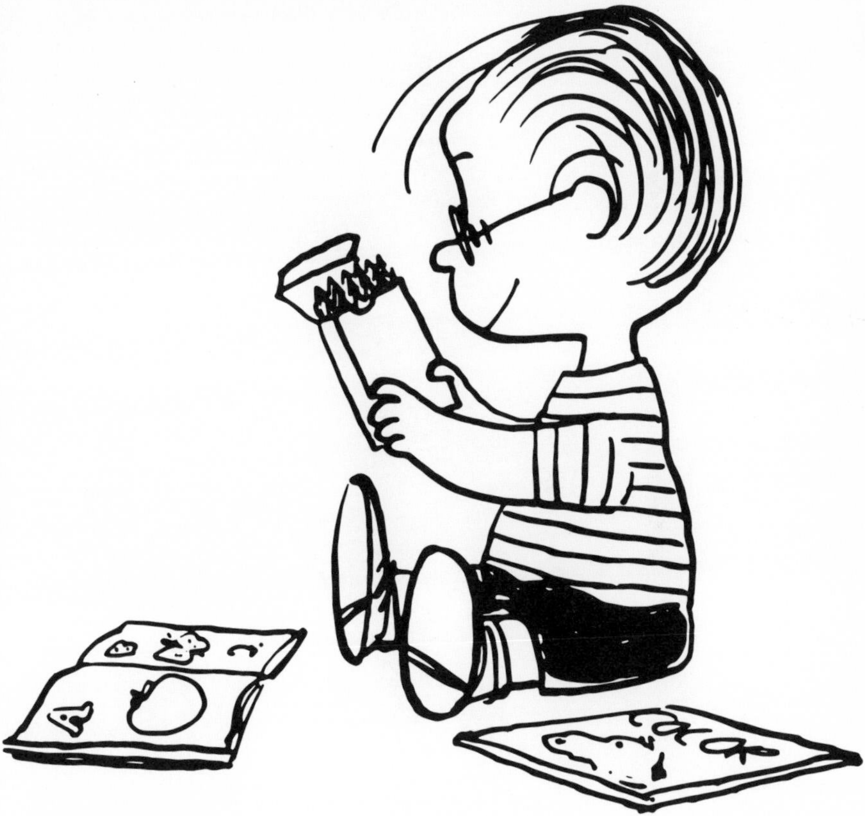

**Happiness is
a piece of fudge caught
on the first bounce.**

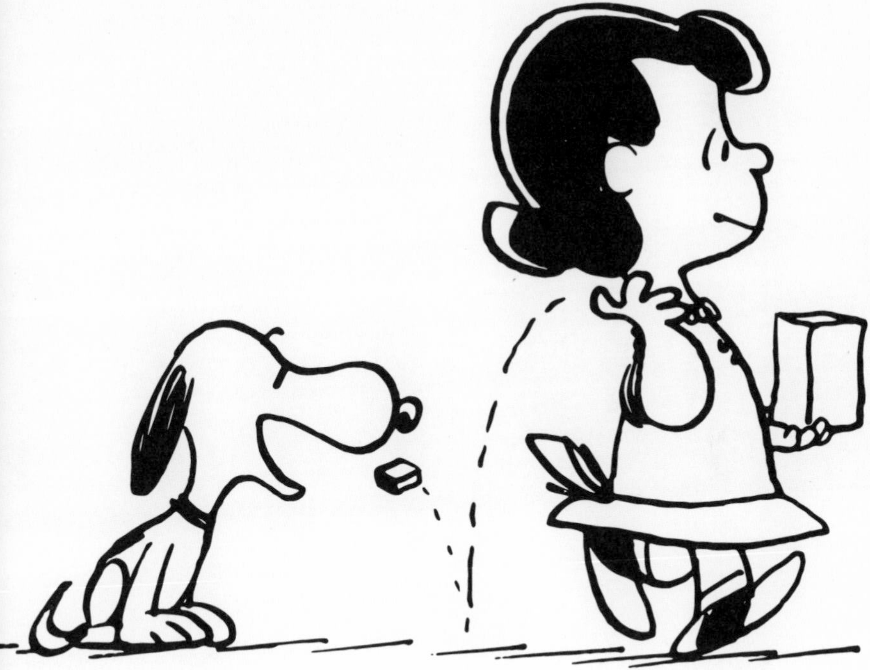

Happiness is
finding the little piece
with the pink edge and
part of the sky and the
top of the sailboat.

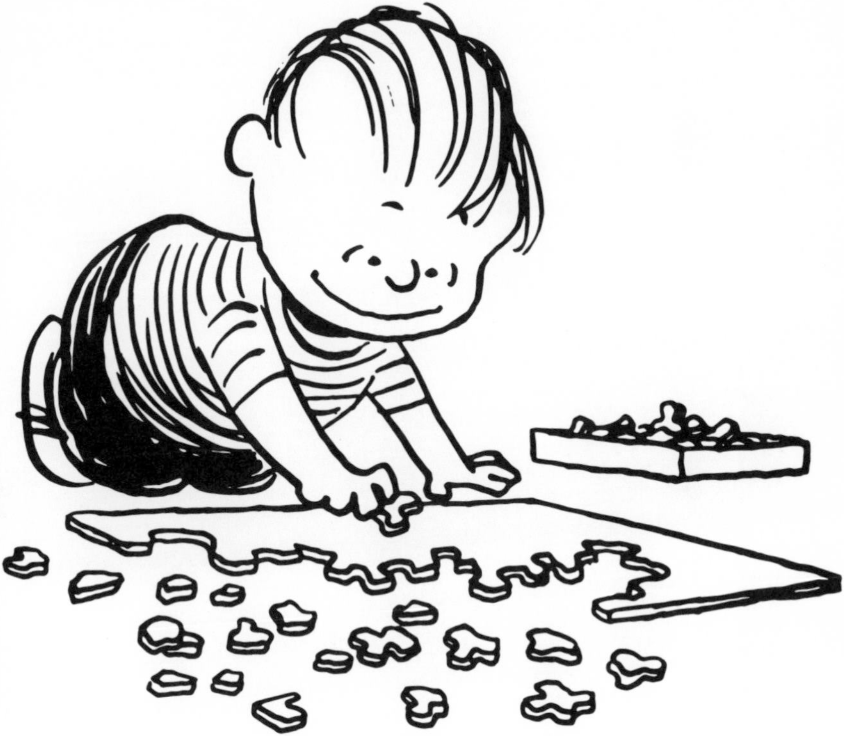

Happiness is
finding out you're not
so dumb after all.

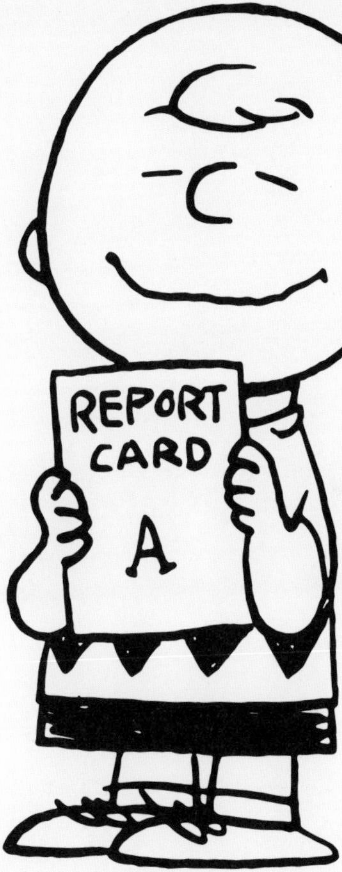
REPORT
CARD
A

Happiness is thirty-five cents for the movie, fifteen cents for popcorn and a nickel for a candy bar.

**Happiness is
one thing to one person
and another thing to
another person.**

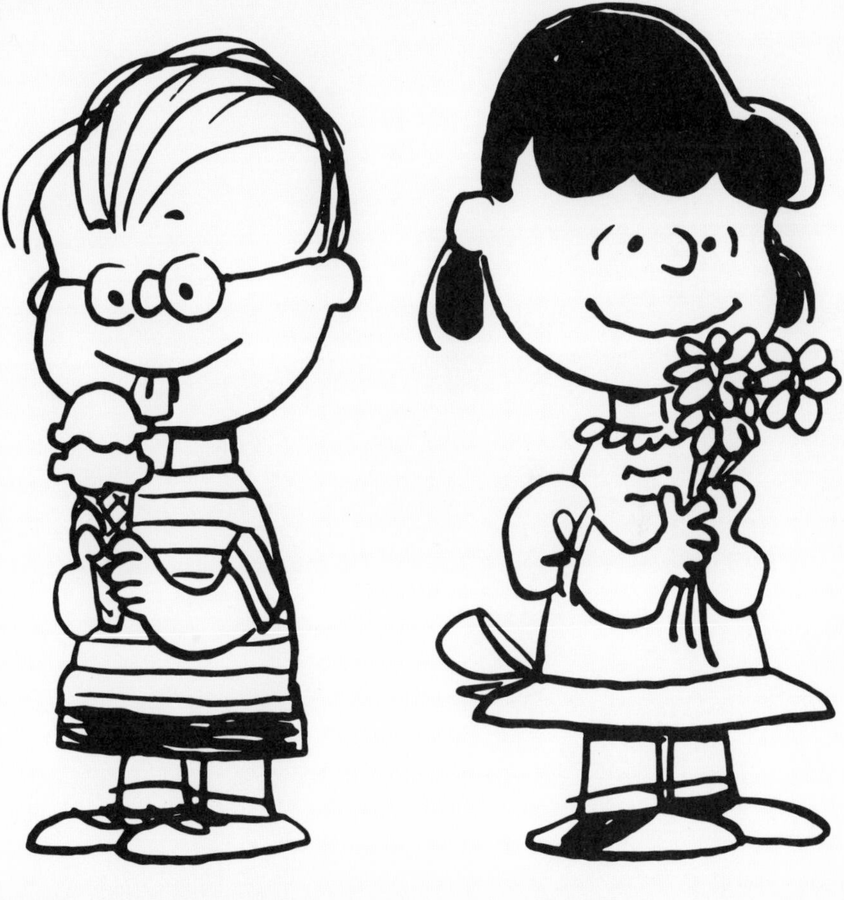

ABOUT CIDER MILL PRESS BOOK PUBLISHERS

Good ideas ripen with time. From seed to harvest, Cider Mill Press brings fine reading, information, and entertainment together between the covers of its creatively crafted books. Our Cider Mill bears fruit twice a year, publishing a new crop of titles each spring and fall.

CIDER MILL
PRESS
BOOK
PUBLISHERS

VISIT US ON THE WEB AT

www.cidermillpress.com

OR WRITE TO US AT

12 Spring Street
PO Box 454
Kennebunkport, Maine 04046

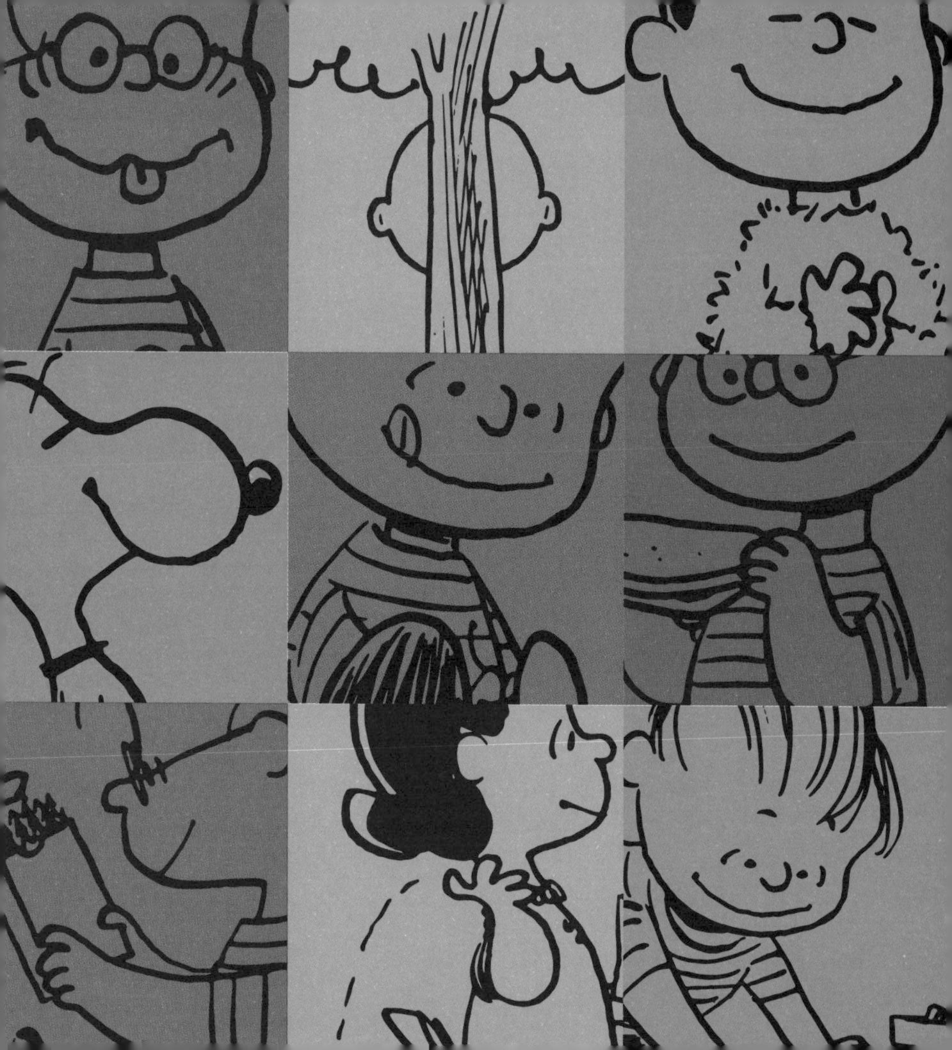

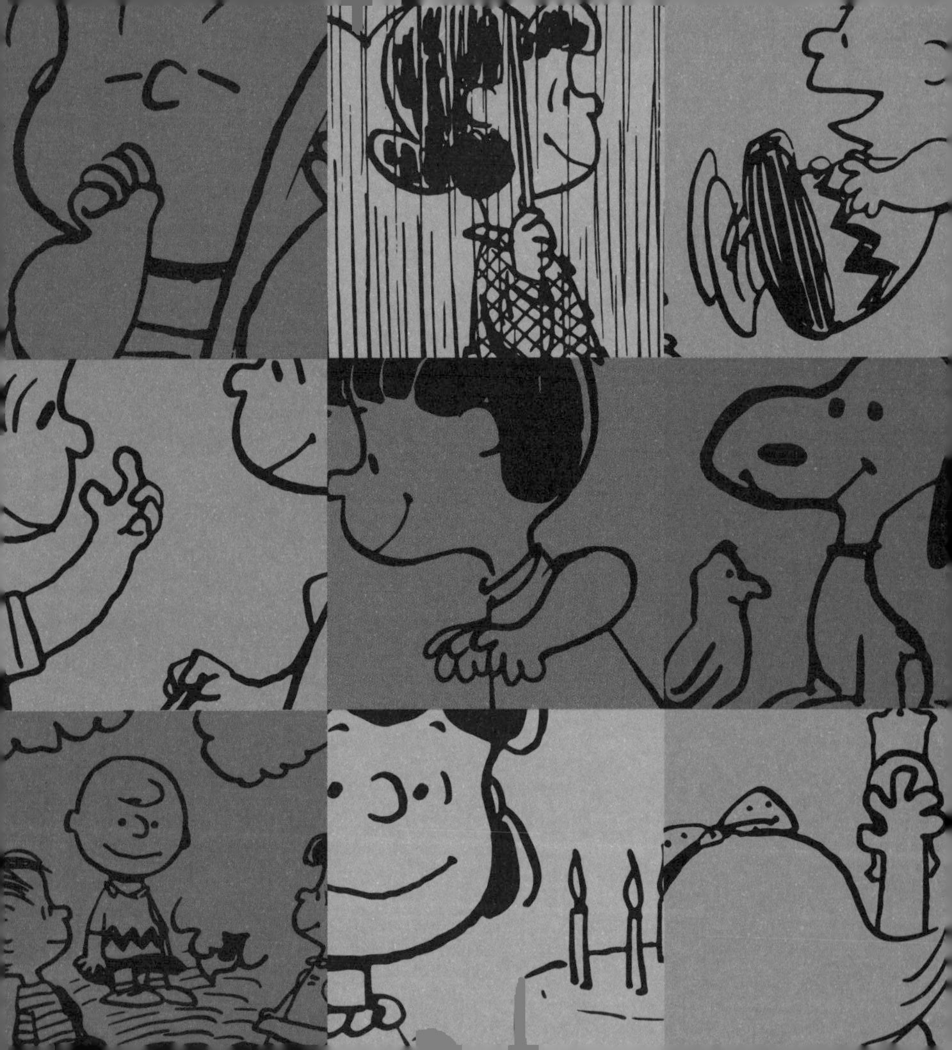